MW00900358

The Parrots and Papa Bois

Lynette Comissiong

For Merrydale, Paula-Anne and Jonathon

Marcus and Mira flew all over the Talparo forest on a tiny island in the blue Caribbean Sea.

'Cra-cra-cra-aa.
Craaa, craaa, craaa craaa,' they squawked.

Everywhere they went all the animals complained about the raucous noise they made.

Fergie Frog was trying to sleep.

'Kiddip, kiddipp, kiddip, kidipp.
Go away, go away!' he croaked.

Susie Squirrel didn't like the noise either. Every time Marcus and Mira squawked, her babies cried.

Bertie Cricket just hid under a large bois cano leaf.

One day Thera Thrush rested on a branch near to Mira. Thera sang so sweetly.

'Cheeroo,
cheeroo,
cheeroo.
Chi, chi, chi, chi.'

Mira cocked her head and listened.

'I wish I could sing sweet like Thera,' she told Marcus. But all she could say was,

'Cra-aa, cra, cra-ak cra-aa.'

Marcus ruffled his feathers and flew closer to Mira, but that did not comfort her.

Mira saw Suzie Squirrel under the trees. She was gathering seeds. Mira spread her wings and swooped down.

'Cra-aa cra-ak, cra-aa.
Tell me how to sing sweet like Thera,' she begged.

Suzie put down her seeds.

'Tut, tut, tut, tut, tut, tut, tut.

Drink honey and lime for one whole week.
Your voice will be sweet when you open your beak,'
she squeaked.

Mira flew at once to Issa's hive to get some honey.

Every morning for one whole week she drank honey and lime. But that didn't help. When she opened her beak all she could say was, 'Cra-aa, cra-aak.'

She was not happy at all.

Next she saw Fergie Frog sitting on a twig in the pond.

She swooped down

and rested on a big stone

on the side of the pond.

'Cra-aa craak, craa.
*Tell me how to sing
sweet like Thera,'*
she begged Fergie.

Fergie yawned,

'Kiddip, kiddip, kiddip, kiddip, kiddip, kiddip.'
Sleep till twelve o'clock for one whole week.
Your voice will be sweet when you open your beak,'

Fergie told her.

Fergie was really annoyed with Mira. She woke him up at six o'clock every morning with her raucous 'Cra-craa-craa'.

Mira slept till twelve o'clock for one whole week. Fergie and all the other night creatures were glad.

But that didn't help. When she opened her beak all she could say was, 'Cra-aa, craa aak'. She wasn't happy at all.

Mira grew sadder and sadder. She wanted to sing sweet, like Thera.

Marcus wanted to cheer her up.

'Cra, aa aa, craa craa.
Will you come with me to find ripe bananas, please?'
he asked her.

Mira shook her head.

'Craaa cra cra.
Ripe paw-paw?'

Mira shook her head.

'Craa craa.
'Ripe mangoes?'

Mira still shook her head.

Marcus could not persuade her to go with him at all.

Mira sat on a branch all day long. She watched Thera flying about, singing in her sweet voice,

'Cheeroo, cheeroo, cheeroo.
Chi, chi, chi, chi.'

The days went by. Rain fell every day. Lightning flashed and thunder rolled. The forest grew cold and dark. No one heard Marcus and Mira's raucous

'Craa craa craa-aa'.

Suzie Squirrel hid in the trees with her babies.

Fergie Frog slept all day. At night he sang softly,

'Kiddip, kiddip, kiddip.'

Bertie Cricket didn't chirrup. He just hid under a large bois cano leaf.

All the animals were quiet.

After six full moons, the rain stopped and the sun shone bright once again. The noise of all the animals filled the forest.

Once again the animals began to complain about Marcus and Mira's raucous
'Cra craa, cra, cra, craak'.

Mira was still sad. She wanted to sing sweet like Thera.

One morning she saw Bertie Cricket. He was sitting on a large bois cano leaf.

She swooped down.

'Cra-aa, cra-aak, cra-aa.
Bertie, tell me how to sing sweet like Thera,' she begged.

Bertie was frightened. He leapt to a higher leaf.

'Chirrup, chirrup, chirrup.
Chirrup, chirrup, chirruppp.
*Ask Papa Bois to change how you speak.
Your voice will be sweet when you open
your beak,'* he told her.

Early the next morning, Mira flew far into the forest to visit Papa Bois. Papa Bois was old and wise, he was King of the Forest. He knew every animal, every tree, every plant, every flower, every fruit. He knew everything. Papa Bois could even understand all the animals.

'Cra-aa, craak craaa.
Papa Bois, please help me. Please make me sing sweet, like Thera,' Mira cawed.

'You want me to make you sing sweet like Thera?'
When Papa Bois spoke the forest grew quiet.

'Cra-aa craak-cra cra cra-a-a-a.
All the animals always complain about my raucous voice. Every morning they shout, "Shut your beak, Mira, shut your beak!"' sobbed Mira.

Papa Bois shook his head.
'Ah, Mira, you can never sing sweet like Thera, but ...'

Mira didn't wait to hear anything more. She spread her wings and flew away.

That night she could not sleep. She imagined that she heard Thera's sweet song,

At the crack of dawn, Mira flew and flew and flew far into the forest to where all the silk cotton trees grew.

Ma Zeena, the evil witch, watched Mira coming.

'Stop right there!' Ma Zeena cackled, 'What you come here for?'

Ma Zeena didn't like anyone to come close to her house.

Mira was afraid of Ma Zeena.

'Cra, cra-cra-cra aaa, cra.
Ma Zeena, please make me sing sweet like Thera,'
she squawked.

Ma Zeena hobbled out of the house.

'I will make you sing sweeter than Thera,' she said. 'But first you must do something for me. There's a fruit tree near Papa Bois' house. All the fruits of the forest grow on that one tree. Pick one carambola for me and I will make you sing sweeter than Thera.'

Ma Zeena smiled to herself as she watched Mira fly away.

'If I eat that carambola I will be more powerful than Papa Bois. I will rule the forest ... Heh, heh, heh, heh ...' she cackled.

Mira flew at once to Papa Bois' house.

She swooped down

and picked

the carambola.

Suddenly, the forest grew dark.

The winds began to whistle through the trees
and there was a noise like thunder!

Mira was afraid. She dropped the carambola
and flew straight back to Marcus.

She stood on the branch, trembling, and hid her head under her wing.

'Cra, cra, cra, cra, cra-aaaa cra,' Mira cried. She told Marcus exactly what had happened.

'Cra, craaak cra, craak.' Marcus cawed loudly.He was angry with Ma Zeena for fooling Mira. He was angry with Mira for trying to steal Papa Bois' fruit.

Mira felt ashamed.

Marcus flapped his wings and flew close to Mira.

Then together they flew to Papa Bois.

Mira stood in front of Papa Bois and bent her head down. Papa Bois knew exactly what had happened. He knew it was Ma Zeena who wanted his carambola. And he knew why she wanted it.

'Come here.' he said.
Papa Bois patted Mira's head.
'Say after me... "Morning, morning, morning!"'

Mira cawed and cawed in her raucous voice. She tried and tried and tried. Then slowly she began to say the words,

'Craaa, cra, morrrr,
morrrr, mor,
ninggggg, ninnnn,
morrminggggg,
mor, mor, morrgggggg!'

Eventually she said,
'Morning, morning, morning!'

Marcus tried too and they both said,

'Morning, morning, morning!'

Papa Bois smiled and walked off, singing.

Mira never saw Ma Zeena again.

Every time Mira heard Thera's sweet voice, she just smiled.

Every morning, as Mira and Marcus flew in the forest, they called, 'Morning, Morning!'

Not one single animal complained any more.

And that is how, to this day,
you sometimes hear
parrots repeat what you say!

Macmillan Education
Between Towns Road, Oxford OX4 3PP
A division of Macmillan Publishers Limited
Companies and representatives throughout the world

www.macmillan-caribbean.com

ISBN 0-333-93062-2

First published 2001

Designed by Rai & Quantrill
Illustrated by Avril Turner
Cover design by Rai & Quantrill
Cover illustration by Avril Turner

Colour separation by Tenon & Polert Colour Scanning Ltd

Printed in China

2005 2004 2003 2002 2001
10 9 8 7 6 5 4 3 2 1